MONSTER HUNTER

YETI

STEVE BARLOW AND STEVE SKIDMORE

ILLUSTRATED BY PAUL DAVIDSON

Franklin Watts
First published in Great Britain in 2020
by The Watts Publishing Group

Text © Steve Barlow and Steve Skidmore 2020
Illustrations © The Watts Publishing Group 2020
Cover design: Cathryn Gilbert and Peter Scoulding

ISBN 978 1 4451 6999 6
ebook ISBN 978 1 4451 6998 9
Library ebook ISBN 978 1 4451 6997 2

1 3 5 7 9 10 8 6 4 2

Printed in Great Britain

MIX
Paper from
responsible sources
FSC® C104740
FSC
www.fsc.org

Franklin Watts
An imprint of
Hachette Children's Group
Part of The Watts Publishing Group
Carmelite House
50 Victoria Embankment
London EC4Y 0DZ

Mission Statement

You are the hero of this mission.

Each section of this book is numbered. At the end of most sections, you will have to make a choice. The choice you make will take you to a different section of the book.

Some of your choices will help you to complete the adventure successfully. But if you make the wrong choice, death may be the best you can hope for! Because even dying is better than being UNDEAD and becoming a slave of the monsters you have sworn to destroy!

Dare you go up against a world of monsters?

All right, then.

Let's see what you've got...

Introduction

You are an agent of **G.H.O.S.T.** — Global Headquarters Opposing Supernatural Threats.

Our world is under constant attack from supernatural horrors that lurk in the shadows. It's your job to make sure they stay there.

You have studied all kinds of monsters, and know their habits and behaviour. You are an expert in disguise, able to move among monsters in human form as a spy. You are expert in all forms of martial arts. G.H.O.S.T. has supplied you with weapons, equipment and other assets that make you capable of destroying any supernatural creature.

G.H.O.S.T.

You are based at Arcane Hall, a spooky and secret-laden mansion. Your butler, Cranberry, is another G.H.O.S.T. agent who assists you in all your adventures, providing you with information and backup.

Your life at Arcane Hall is comfortable and peaceful; but you know that at any moment, the G.H.O.S.T. High Command can order you into action in any part of the world...

Go to 1.

You are on a G.H.O.S.T. training exercise in the Arctic Circle. You are driving a snowmobile across the ice, heading for a rendezvous point with a local Inuit agent.

The going is tough as the frozen sea ice is uneven and the wind whips up the snow, making visibility almost zero.

Suddenly the ice in front of you cracks and splits apart. There is no time to avoid it and you are thrown from the snowmobile onto the ice. The vehicle falls into the crevasse and with it all your survival gear and weapons!

You hear a growl and, peering through the swirling ice, you make out the outline of a giant polar bear heading your way. You know if you activate your distress signal, you will fail the training exercise, but the bear is fast approaching and you need a weapon.

To climb into the crevasse and rescue your equipment, go to 37.

To activate your distress signal, go to 45.

2

You aim your BAM gun and manage to take out a couple of the attacking yetis before they reach you. But your situation is hopeless. There are too many to deal with and they are too quick for you. You take out another creature before the leading yeti reaches you and smashes you to the floor.

Go to 42.

3

You land the helicopter.

"No sign of the yeti," you say. You pick up your BAM (Blast All Monsters) gun and step out of the helicopter.

At that moment the air is filled with a screeching howl.

"Agent!" shouts Cranberry.

But his warning comes too late. You turn to see a creature from your worst nightmares running at supernatural speed towards you. Before you can aim your weapon, the yeti smashes into you, sending you flying...

Go to 42.

4

As the yeti tries to grab hold of you, you reach for your YO gun and pull the trigger. At such point-blank range, you can't miss and the creature drops down dead.

"Well the tracker idea isn't going to work now," says Cranberry. "And we can't keep flying around aimlessly. We're running out of fuel."

To explore the area now, go to 35.
To head back and refuel, go to 21.

"So what's the mission?" you ask.

"We have a problem with yetis," replies the DG.

You are surprised. "Yetis? I thought that they were just make-believe creatures — the abominable snowmen of legend."

"That's what we want people to believe," replies the DG. "Yetis are more than abominable — they're deadly! Have you heard of Bhutan?"

"Of course!" you reply. "It's a country in Asia."

"Very good. We need you there ASAP. I'll send a mission briefing when you're on the Phantom Flyer."

The screen changes to show a map of Bhutan.

"Yetis? Interesting," says Cranberry. "Agent, I suggest we stop off at Arcane Hall to pick up some new weapons I've been developing. I think we're going to need them."

To agree with Cranberry go to 31.

To disagree and head straight to Bhutan, go to 20.

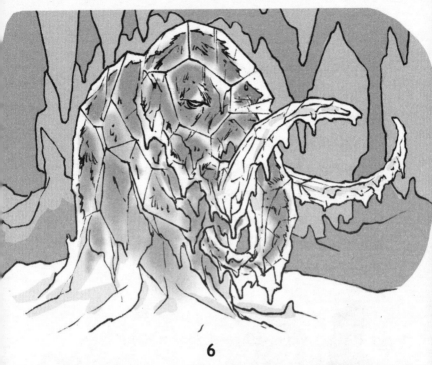

6

You fire a barrage of grenades around the cavern, making sure that you aren't in the range of the nitrogen gas cloud.

The yetis and the mammoths come to a sudden halt as they are instantly frozen. You continue to fire until you have no ammunition left and all your attackers are big lumps of ice!

You turn and head down the tunnel.

Go to 50.

You are soon heading towards the glacial valley.

"Do we have an exact spot for the lair?" you ask Taru.

"No," she replies. "We'll just have to fly around and hopefully your MAAD can locate it."

Cranberry pilots the helicopter up and down the valley, whilst you point your MAAD out of the window. But the search is futile. There is no sign of any yetis.

Suddenly, a red light flashes on the helicopter's control board.

"What's that warning light for?" you ask.

"We're running out of fuel," Cranberry replies. "We have to go back to the airport."

To head back to the airport, go to 21.
To keep searching for the lair, go to 35.

8

You throw down the weapons, quickly grab hold of two ice picks and use them to climb up the rapidly closing walls of ice.

You manage to reach the top of the crevasse and pull yourself out just as the ice walls crash together. You lie, exhausted, before a loud roar brings you back to your senses.

You are weaponless and the bear is still there!

To try to scare away the bear, go to 15.
To activate your distress signal, go to 45.

9

You decide to investigate the opening before calling for backup.

You move forward, but come to a sudden halt. You see a creature from prehistory standing 30 metres ahead.

It's a sabre-toothed tiger! It must have been released from its underground habitat when the yetis' lair opened up. It sees you and pads towards you, growling...

To use the BAM gun, go to 41.
To use the NAY, go to 25.

10

You move carefully through the monastery's entrance gate.

Suddenly, the air is filled with a nightmarish howl. You see a figure leaping at supernatural speed towards you.

You pull the trigger of the BAM gun, but miss the moving target! The creature smashes into you, sending you sprawling to the ground.

Go to 42.

You realise that you have to take out the yeti silently and as quickly as possible, before it warns any others. So you choose your YO laser gun. You take aim through the telescopic sight and pull the trigger. The laser hits the creature and it drops to the floor.

You speed towards the opening, light a glow stick and make your way into a tunnel lined with ice. Ahead, you can hear howling. You ready your BAM weapon and move forward.

Go to 30.

12

"We'll take the Spook Truck," you say.

Taru shakes her head. "That is not possible. The yetis' lair is supposedly underneath a melting glacier. There's no way we can drive there."

"Perhaps we should listen to someone who has local knowledge," says Cranberry.

You realise he is right.

Go to 34.

13

The helicopter heads towards the glacial valley where you think the yetis' lair is located.

You keep a careful eye on your 'passenger' to make sure it doesn't wake up. Soon you are flying over the ice-covered valleys and mountains of the Eastern Himalayas.

"We need to drop off our hairy friend," you say.

"Should we go further up the mountain, or down into one of the valleys?" Cranberry asks.

To go down into the valley, go to 21.
To head further up the mountain, go to 44.

14

As you turn on the MAAD, a nightmarish howl echoes around the monastery. You point the MAAD towards one of the several temples that make up the complex.

It starts flashing red — you've located the yeti!

If you picked up the specialist weapons from Arcane Hall on your way to Bhutan, go to 39.

If you didn't, go to 24.

15

The bear moves towards you as you begin jumping and shouting to try to scare it away.

The tactic works as the bear comes to a halt a few metres ahead of you. Then it opens its great jaws and gives a huge roar.

You clench your fists and ready yourself for the bear's attack.

It stops roaring and you are amazed to see the side of the 'bear' slide open. A familiar-looking figure steps out. "Hello, Agent. Need some help?"

It's Cranberry!

Go to 26.

The yeti leaps at you, but you grab hold of its arm and fling it out of the open door.

It drops to the ground, and stares back up at you before sprinting away.

Your radio tracker begins to flash red. "It's working!" says Taru.

"Hopefully it's heading home," you reply. "Follow that yeti!"

"We're running out of fuel, Agent," warns Cranberry. "Either you follow it on foot, or we head back to the airport, refuel and come back."

To stay in the helicopter and refuel,
go to 21.

To follow the yeti on foot, go to 38.

17

"Let's hope the SAY is as good as you say," you
tell Cranberry.

"Oh very droll, Agent," he replies and passes
the rifle. You load a tranquilliser dart and aim it
at the entrance to the temple.

Another howl echoes through the monastery.
Then the yeti bursts from the doorway heading
towards you at supernatural speed.

You pull the trigger and score a direct hit. Nothing happens and the yeti continues heading towards you, jaws open revealing razor-sharp teeth.

You reach for your BAM gun but the yeti is nearly upon you! It reaches out...

...and drops to the floor, stunned.

You take a deep breath. "You need to work on getting the knock-out dosage right, Cranberry," you say.

"Now what do we do with it?" asks Taru.

To load the yeti onto the helicopter, go to 33.

To send it to G.H.O.S.T. HQ for examination, go to 49.

18

"OK, let's get to the monastery and find this yeti, so we can see what we're up against," you say.

You load the helicopter with the equipment you'll need and take to the air.

Forty minutes later, the monastery is in view. Taru points out a group of monks fleeing from

one of the monastery buildings towards the
local village.

To land in the village, go to 29.
To land inside the monastery, go to 3.

19

You aim the YO weapon at the ice roof and let loose several laser blasts.

The roof disintegrates and huge blocks of ice crash down. The mammoths are startled and stampede, crushing several yetis as they rampage through the cavern. Other yetis are crushed by the falling roof.

But you have only bought yourself a brief respite. The yetis regroup and head towards you.

To try and escape down the tunnel, go to 36.

To use the NAY grenade gun, go to 6.

20

"You heard the DG, Cranberry," you say. "We have to get to Bhutan ASAP. I'm afraid we don't have time to pick up some experimental weapons."

"Very well," replies Cranberry, "If you're 100 per cent certain, Agent. I just hope you don't regret it later on..."

To change your mind and get the weapons, go to 31.

To go straight to Bhutan, go to 48.

21

You head back down the valley as dark clouds begin to gather. A violent thunderstorm soon breaks out, buffeting the helicopter.

"This is why Bhutan is known as the Land of the Thunder Dragon," Taru tells you.

"Very apt!" you say.

The helicopter spins violently in the storm.

"I can't control it," warns Cranberry.

"Let me take over," you say.

As you undo your seat belt and reach for the controls, a lightning bolt hits the helicopter. The rotors stop dead and the helicopter plunges downwards. As the helicopter crash-lands, you are flung against the window and you black out.

Go to 28.

22

The yeti is moving quickly up the glacier, so you hurry after it. The going is tough, but your Arctic training has helped you prepare for this.

Eventually the tracker indicates that the yeti has stopped moving.

You head towards the edge of the glacier

and take out your binoculars to check out the
landscape. You see a large opening in the rock.
Maybe that's the lair, you think.

To head towards the opening, go to 9.
To call Cranberry for backup, go to 32.

23

"We need to find the lair and deal with that," you say.

"But it's a Code Magenta, which is the highest level of operation," Cranberry says.

"And so is finding the lair!" you snap. "We're heading to the valley."

Taru is not happy. "I am going to the monastery," she says, "and I'm taking the helicopter!"

To stop her, go to 43.

To change your mind and go to the monastery, go to 18.

24

You ready your BAM gun and signal to Cranberry and Taru that you are moving in.

As you make your way towards the building, another howl rents the air. Then a figure bursts from the doorway heading towards you at supernatural speed. But you are ready for the creature's attack. You pull the trigger of the BAM and score a direct hit.

The yeti howls in pain, opening its jaws

to reveal rows of razor-sharp teeth, before slumping to the ground. Cranberry and the local agent hurry over and view the lifeless creature. "Abominable indeed," says Cranberry.

You check the monastery with the MAAD to make sure there are no more yetis lurking around, but the results are negative.

"Let's find the yetis' lair," you say.

Go to 7.

25

You ready the NAY grenade launcher and pull the trigger. A grenade explodes in front of the tiger releasing a cloud of nitrogen gas that freezes the prehistoric creature before it can attack.

Cool, you think. *In fact, frozen...*

You continue to head towards the opening and spy a yeti standing in front of it.

This must be the lair, you think.

To shoot the yeti with your BAM gun, go to 41.

To use the SAY rifle, go to 46.

To use the YO laser gun, go to 11.

"What are you doing here and why are you inside that thing?" you ask Cranberry.

"This is a spy device G.H.O.S.T. employs in Arctic regions," he explains. "I was ordered to use it and follow your training mission progress. It certainly fooled you!"

"I knew it was fake all along," you say unconvincingly.

"I believe you, Agent," he replies, also unconvincingly. "I'll order up a helicopter; the Director General has a mission for you."

Soon you are sitting in a G.H.O.S.T. helicopter heading back towards land. The comms screen lights up revealing the face of the Director General. "I've heard you had a mishap with a snowmobile," she says.

"I was surprised that the ice broke up like it did," you explain.

"A consequence of climate change and global warming," she replies. "The Arctic ice covering is melting and getting thinner. It's not the only place to suffer from global warming.

Glaciers around the world are shrinking and as a consequence of this, we have a job for you."

I'm a hunter of the supernatural, you think, *not an eco-warrior!*

To ask for a different mission, go to 40.
To listen to what the DG has to say, go to 5.

27

You grab hold of the NAY grenade launcher.

"No!" shouts Cranberry, but his warning comes too late as you pull the trigger.

The grenade explodes, releasing a cloud of high purity nitrogen gas inside the helicopter. The yeti is frozen solid, but so are you, Taru and Cranberry!

Without a pilot, the helicopter drops from the sky onto the glacier and explodes.

That brain freeze didn't help!
Go back to 1.

28

You come to, and hear a deep growl above you. Your heart misses a beat as you look up to see a pack of yetis staring at you, claws out and teeth bared.

You didn't find the yetis — they found you!

Looks like you're in time for dinner. Sadly, the dinner is YOU!

Go back to 1.

"We'll land in the village," you tell Cranberry.

Minutes later you are on the ground and heading up the slope towards the monastery entrance, BAM (Blasts All Monsters) gun at the ready. Cranberry and Taru follow.

You reach the entrance but there is no sign of the yeti.

To use your MAAD (Monster and Alien Detector), go to 14.

To head inside, go to 10.

Soon the tunnel opens up and you find yourself at the edge of a vast cavern, which is lit up by ice crystals glowing red and blue. Dozens of yetis prowl around and you are amazed to see a herd of woolly mammoths drinking from a large pool in the middle of the cavern.

As you take in the scene, a yeti crouching away to your left sniffs at the air and gives a howl. Soon all the yetis are sniffing and turning their heads to where you are standing. They've picked up your scent.

As one, they begin to move towards you!

To use your BAM to shoot at the yetis, go to 2.

To use your YO gun to shoot at the ice roof, go to 19.

"Are they necessary for this mission, Cranberry?" you ask.

"Oh yes, Agent. They'll be just perfect."

"OK, let's get them."

Later that day you are in the lab at Arcane Hall where Cranberry shows you his new inventions. "This laser gun is a Yeti Obliterator," he says.

You laugh. "The YO weapon! Are you kidding me?"

"No, Agent, it isn't a laughing matter, certainly not for the yetis. It fires a laser beam mixed with infrared light, which cuts through their hide. Normal laser beams don't work on them. "

He hands you a stubby looking gun. "And this device is called Neutralise All Yetis."

"NAY? You really need to work on the names, Cranberry. What does it do?"

"It fires grenades that release a high purity nitrogen gas cloud. It will freeze everything in a 10-metre radius. Finally, there is this SAY dart rifle."

"SAY, what?"

"Exactly Agent, SAY — Stuns All Yetis. It works well on individual creatures. It knocks them out for a couple of hours or so."

You are impressed. "Well, let's go and hunt some yetis!"

Go to 48.

32

You try and contact Cranberry on your comms link, but the signal is weak.

As you attempt to raise Cranberry again, you hear a growl coming from behind you. You turn and your heart misses a beat. Standing before you is a sabre-toothed tiger!

How on earth...? is your last thought as the prehistoric creature pounces and you feel its razor-sharp teeth rip into your jugular vein, releasing your precious lifeblood.

It was behind you! Go back to 1.

33

"We'll take the yeti with us," you say.

Cranberry and Taru looked shocked. "Are you thinking quite right?" asks the butler.

"I've got an idea," you reply.

"Is this idea of yours a good one or a bad one?" replies Cranberry.

"Time will tell. Let's tie this bad boy up and head off."

Soon the bound and unconscious yeti is on board the helicopter. You take out a syringe and insert a microchip GPS tracker under the creature's skin. "It's a special Radio Frequency Identification implant," you explain. "We leave the yeti on the glacier and when it wakes up, it might lead us to the lair."

"Impressive thinking," says Taru.

"Please don't encourage the agent, it will only go to his head," says Cranberry as he takes the controls and the helicopter lifts up and off.

Go to 13.

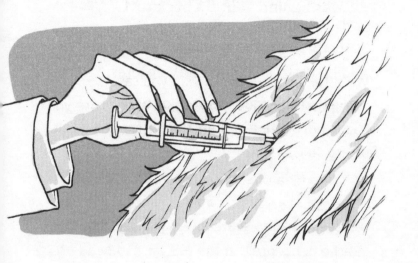

34

"Tell me more about the yetis' lair," you say to Taru.

"It's in a glacial valley near a mountain called Ghangkar Puensam, which is thought to be the highest mountain in the world that's never been climbed. The only way we can get there is by helicopter."

"Then let's load up the helicopter with equipment from the Spook Truck and get going."

At that moment your comms link bursts into life. "Code Magenta alert! Reported sighting of a yeti at the Gangteng Monastery. G.H.O.S.T. agents, scramble!"

"That's about 140 km away," says Taru. "We could be there in around forty minutes."

To go to the monastery, go to 18.

To ignore the alert and head for the yetis' lair, go to 23.

35

"We need to keep searching," you say. "We can land the helicopter on the glacier and head off on foot."

"I hope you know what you're doing," says Cranberry. He lands the 'copter on the glacier. You load up your equipment and set off across the glacier.

Hours pass, but you find nothing. You report your location back to HQ, where the DG is not impressed. "While you've been wasting time dancing on ice, the yetis have been discovered miles away," she snaps. "You need to get going immediately!"

You make your way back to the helicopter, knowing that you will have to refuel before you go yeti hunting.

Go to 21.

36

You turn and race down the tunnel, screaming into your comms link for Cranberry. But there is no signal.

The howls of the yetis get closer. There's no way you can outrun them — you're going to have to fight! You spin round, BAM gun ready.

Go to 2.

37

As the bear moves towards you, you slide down the ice wall of the crevasse. You reach the stricken snowmobile and start to unload the equipment.

As you are gathering your weapons, there is a loud crack and the ice begins to move.

The walls of the crevasse close in on you. You're going to be crushed unless you act quickly!

To try to climb out, go to 8.

To activate your distress signal, go to 45.

38

"We haven't got time to mess around," you say. "Drop me here, Cranberry. You and Taru go back and refuel. Then round up some more G.H.O.S.T. agents. We might need them!"

Cranberry lands the helicopter as you check out your equipment. You step onto the glacier and watch as the helicopter takes off.

You give a see-you-later-hopefully wave and look at your tracker. The yeti is on the move!

Go to 22.

39

"Let's try out these weapons of yours," you say to Cranberry.

"I was hoping you'd give them a whirl," he replies. "Which one do you want to use? I suggest the Yeti Obliterator or the Stuns All Yetis," says Cranberry. "Kill it or knock it out!"

To choose the YO gun, go to 47.
To choose the SAY rifle, go to 17.

40

"Is there another mission I can have?" you say. "I don't think my job includes solving the planet's environmental problems. I hunt monsters and stop them being problems."

The DG is furious. "Your first problem is that you speak before you think. Your second problem is that you don't know what the mission is, and your third and biggest problem is me! I'm your boss so listen to what I have to say and don't interrupt!"

"Sorry," you mumble.

Go to 5.

41

You blast the creature with several shots and it drops down dead. But the noise of the BAM gun echoes round the valley.

A series of loud cracks above you makes you look up. You see the snow and ice on the mountainside breaking. You've caused an avalanche!

Desperately, you run towards the shelter of an overhanging outcrop, but you are too slow. A block of ice hits you and you crash to the ground, unconscious.

Go to 28.

42

You lie on the floor, helpless. The yeti stands over you before it opens its slavering jaws, revealing deadly razor-sharp teeth.

The last sound you hear is its victorious howl, before the yeti's jaws crunch down on your neck...

Ouch! Go back to 1.

43

You take out a gun and point it at Taru. "I'm taking the helicopter!"

In reply, Taru suddenly spins around and leaps at you, kung-fu style! She catches your jaw with a perfect hammer kick and you drop to the floor, unconscious.

Hours later you wake up to find yourself on your own. There is a written note pinned to your coat.

Gone to save the world.
— Cranberry

P.S. The D.G. says
you're sacked.

That's a kick in the teeth! Go back to 1.

"I think the lair is more likely to be located further up the mountain," you say.

"Very well, Agent," Cranberry says. "Let's see if your hunch is right."

He turns the helicopter towards the looming peaks of the Himalayas and soon you are passing over a great mass of ice.

"That's one of the glaciers that is melting," says Taru. "You can see some of the mountain that has been revealed at the sides."

"Maybe that's where the lair has been opened up," you say. "Let's drop off our passenger and see what happens."

You open the door.

As you do so, you hear a low growl. The yeti has woken up!

It strains at its bonds, breaks them apart and turns towards you, ready to pounce.

To blast it with the YO gun, go to 4.

To use the NAY weapon, go to 27.

To push the yeti out of the door, go to 16.

45

You activate your distress signal on your smart watch.

A message flashes up on it. "Agent failed. Contract terminated."

Seemingly from nowhere, a helicopter appears and hovers above you. A G.H.O.S.T. agent lowers a rope ladder.

"Climb up, Agent ... or should I say ex-agent? The Director General says G.H.O.S.T. doesn't need people who give in straight away..."

What were you thinking of? Sort yourself out and go back to 1.

46

You ready the SAY rifle, take aim and pull the trigger. Through the telescopic sight, you see the yeti's head jerk up and it gives a howl. Then it turns and disappears into the lair.

You curse your choice of weapon — the knock-out drug doesn't work immediately! Seconds later, a dozen yetis appear from the opening and head towards you at supernatural speed.

Go to 2.

47

"We'll go with the YO," you say.

Cranberry hands it over. "Set it to full blast," he says. "There's no point in taking any chances."

Another howl erupts from the temple and a figure emerges from the entrance. It moves at supernatural speed towards you.

You pull the YO trigger and a laser beam shoots out, hitting the yeti in the chest. The creature stops dead in its tracks. You shoot another beam and the yeti drops lifeless to the ground, its fur smouldering from the laser beams.

You check the monastery with the MAAD to make sure there are no more yetis lurking around, but the results are negative.

"Let's find this yeti lair," you say.

Go to 7.

48

Soon you and Cranberry are in the Phantom Flyer, heading for Bhutan.

The DG sends the mission briefing through:

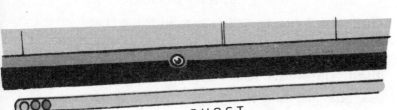

G.H.O.S.T.
CODE MAGENTA – HIGHEST OPERATION LEVEL
ULTRA TOP SECRET

YETIS
SPECIES: Proto-human life form
LIVED: Millions of years ago
LOCATION: Underground caverns beneath HIMALAYAS
DIET: Carnivorous (all meat including HUMAN)
HISTORY: During the last Ice Age (PLEISTOCENE PERIOD: 2.5 million–11,700 years ago), YETIS retreated to underground caverns in the Himalayas and were thought to have frozen to death and become extinct. This is wrong – they seem to have been cryogenically frozen.
CURRENT SITUATION: Global warming has caused glaciers to melt and this has thawed the YETIS. Their lair has also been opened up by the retreating glaciers.
Recent reports from local operatives in Bhutan of Yetis breaking out of the lair and attacking humans.
MISSION OBJECTIVE: Locate the YETIS' lair and DEAL with them.

"Global warming has a lot to answer for, Cranberry," you say. "It's a good thing that the Phantom Flyer uses hydrogen fuel cells for propulsion, otherwise we'd be adding big-time to global warming using a jet! Thank goodness for our cutting-edge, top-secret G.H.O.S.T. technology."

"Quite so, Agent," replies Cranberry. "It's not just supernatural beings that threaten our world with destruction!"

After some hours, the flyer enters Bhutan airspace and you land at an airport in the foothills of the Himalayas.

A local G.H.O.S.T. agent is waiting for you with a Spook Truck and a helicopter. She introduces herself. "My name is Taru. Welcome to Bhutan. I'm here to help you with the mission."

If you wish to find out more about the mission from the agent, go to 34.

If you wish to head off immediately, go to 12.

"We'll get in a local G.H.O.S.T. team to take it and examine it back at HQ."

Taru makes the arrangements and soon the unconscious yeti is secure in a Spook Truck, heading for G.H.O.S.T. HQ.

"Right, let's try and find this yeti lair," you say, as you board the helicopter.

"Head North," you tell Cranberry.

He fires up the engines and, seconds later, you are in the air.

Go to 7.

50

You emerge into the light to see Cranberry standing next to the G.H.O.S.T. helicopter, refuelled and ready to go.

"Had fun, Agent?" he asks.

"I had a very cool experience," you reply.

You contact the DG and recount your adventure.

"We'll get G.H.O.S.T to make the cavern a permanent cryogenic area to keep them frozen and seal up the entrance," she says. "We'll also get Taru and the local agents in Bhutan to hunt for further entrances to the lair. That should cover it all. Well done, Agent." She signs off.

"What now?" asks Cranberry.

"Back home," you reply. "I need to chill!"

EQUIPMENT

Phantom Flyer: For fast international and intercontinental travel, you use the Phantom Flyer, a supersonic business jet crammed full of detection and communication equipment and weaponry.

Spook Trucks: For more local travel you use one of G.H.O.S.T.'s fleet of Spook Trucks — heavily armed and armoured SUVs you requisition from local agents.

MAAD (Monster and Alien Detector)

SAY (Stuns All Yetis)

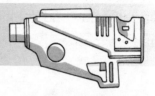

YO (Yeti Obliviator)

NAY (Neutralise All Yetis)

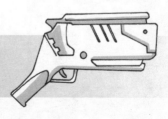

MONSTER HUNTER

I HERO

ROBOT

STEVE BARLOW ◇ STEVE SKIDMORE
Illustrated by PAUL DAVIDSON

1

You are in Arcane Manor reading Mary Shelley's *Frankenstein*. As Cranberry comes in, you drop the book on the floor.

"Aren't you enjoying the story, Agent?" asks Cranberry.

"It's nonsense," you complain. "A scientist creates an intelligent creature that turns on him — it couldn't happen."

"Hmmm." Cranberry hands you a mobile phone. "There's a video call for you from EXOCORP — a cybernetics company based in Silicon Valley, California, USA."

A young woman peers out of the phone screen. She looks very worried.

"I'm Project Director Annick of EXOCORP," she says. "We have a problem with a computer interface on one of our human/robot hybrids..."

Continue the adventure in:

MONSTER HUNTER

ROBOT

About the 2Steves

"The 2Steves" are one
of Britain's most popular
writing double acts for
young people, specialising
in comedy and adventure.

Together they have written many books, including the
I HERO Immortals series.

Find out what they've been up to at:
www.the2steves.net

About the illustrator:
Paul Davidson

Paul Davidson is a British
illustrator and comic book artist.

Have you completed these I HERO adventures?

I HERO Immortals — more to enjoy!

Dinosaur Hunter
Steve Barlow – Steve Skidmore
Illustrated by Judit Tondora

978 1 4451 6963 7 pb
978 1 4451 6964 4 ebook

Fairy
Steve Barlow – Steve Skidmore
Illustrated by Judit Tondora

978 1 4451 6969 9 pb
978 1 4451 6971 2 ebook

Knight
Steve Barlow – Steve Skidmore
Illustrated by Judit Tondora

978 1 4451 6957 6 pb
978 1 4451 6959 0 ebook

Pirate Queen
Steve Barlow – Steve Skidmore
Illustrated by Judit Tondora

978 1 4451 6954 5 pb
978 1 4451 6955 2 ebook

Samurai
Steve Barlow – Steve Skidmore
Illustrated by Judit Tondora

978 1 4451 6960 6 pb
978 1 4451 6962 0 ebook

Witch
Steve Barlow – Steve Skidmore
Illustrated by Judit Tondora

978 1 4451 6966 8 pb
978 1 4451 6967 5 ebook

Defeat all the baddies in Toons:

Killer Custard
Steve Barlow · Steve Skidmore

978 1 4451 5930 0 pb
978 1 4451 5931 7 ebook

Robin Hamster
Steve Barlow · Steve Skidmore

978 1 4451 5921 8 pb
978 1 4451 5922 5 ebook

Enter the Penguin
Steve Barlow · Steve Skidmore

978 1 4451 5924 9 pb
978 1 4451 5925 6 ebook

Kung Fu Kitten
Steve Barlow · Steve Skidmore

978 1 4451 5918 8 pb
978 1 4451 5919 5 ebook

Also by the 2Steves...

978 1 4451 5985 0

Tip can't believe his luck when he
mysteriously wins tickets to see
his favourite team in the cup final.
But there's a surprise in store ...

978 1 4451 5892 1

Big baddie Mr Butt Hedd is in
hot pursuit of the space cadets and has
tracked them down for Lord Evil. But
can Jet, Tip and Boo Hoo find a way to
escape in a cunning disguise?

978 1 4451 5988 1

Jet and Tip get a new command
from Master Control to intercept
some precious cargo. It's time to
become space pirates!

978 1 4451 5979 9

The goodies intercept a distress
signal and race to the rescue. Then
some eight-legged fiends appear ...
Tip and Jet realise it's a trap!